THE GRYPHON

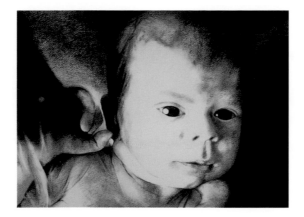

After fleeing their respective lives in London and the Sicmon
Islands, Griffin and Sabine agree to meet in Alexandria. For some
years nothing is heard from either, until a young doctor
receives an unusual postcard from a stranger.

FEB 22

Dear Matthew
It's good to get in touch
with you at last.
We are very impressed with
your general diagnostic abilities.
However we are not convinced
you should be considering
prescribing penicillin for the
Atubi's youngest son.

Write soon – Sabine M. Strohem

And what rough beast...slouches...to be born.

Paolo 25f

DR. MATTHEW SEDON
98 LIVINGSTONE ST.
NAIROBI
KENYA
AIR MAIL

39 La Paz pl. San Rosa
Paolo 9T6

SPECIAL DELIVERY

THE GRYPHON

In Which the Extraordinary Correspondence of
Griffin & Sabine Is Rediscovered

NICK BANTOCK

RAINCOAST BOOKS

Vancouver

This edition first published in Canada in 2001 by

Raincoast Books
9050 Shaughnessy Street
Vancouver, BC
V6P 6E5
(604) 323-7100
www.raincoast.com

First published in the United States in 2001 by Chronicle Books LLC
Book design: Jacqueline Verkley / Byzantium Books Inc.

10 9 8 7 6 5 4 3 2 1

National Library of Canada Cataloguing in Publication Data

Bantock, Nick.
The gryphon

ISBN 1-55192-419-6

1. Imaginary letters. I. Title.
PS8553.A63G79 2001   C813'.54   C2001-910134-1
PR9199.3.B369G79 2001
Raincoast Books gratefully acknowledges the support of the Government of Canada, through the Department of Canadian Heritage and the Book Publishing Industry Development Program.

Printed in Hong Kong

for Paul

The falcon cannot hear the falconer . . .

BREFKORT

Sabine Strohem
You have me at a disadvantage I'm
afraid. I presume that we've been
introduced and my sieve-like memory
has let me down again.

     As for your reference to the
Atubi boy—the idea of employing
penicillin on a 3000-year-old royal
mummy doesn't quite fall within the
practical range of a doctor of
archeology. However, I appreciate
your somewhat sardonic sense of
humor.

     How did you get hold of my
address in Nairobi?
Yours

Sabine Strohem
39 La Paz pl.
San Rosa
Paolo 9T6

VIA AIR MAIL

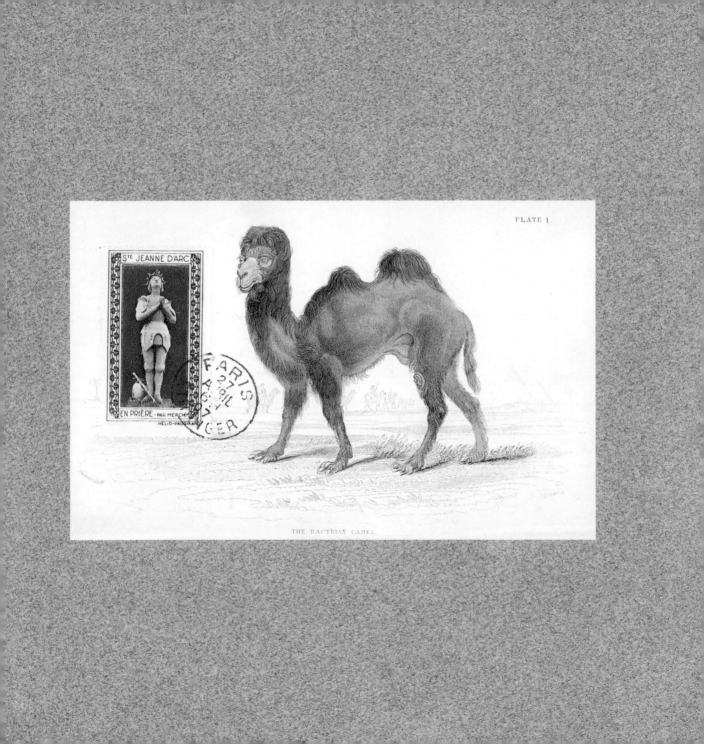

PLATE 1.

THE BACTRIAN CAMEL.

Hello Matthew

How did Kenya work out? Where the masks as interesting as the museum was suggesting?

Today was pure Indian Summer and the boulevards were awash with truanting Parisians extending their breakfasts into their lunches and their lunches into their dinners. Back home in Montreal they'd all get fired, but here ... no one gives a hoot. I've been trying to make the most of the sunshine before classes start again and I put my moleskin on and burrow back into the library's depths. This last year's going to be tough. I can already feel the muscles in my brain tightening in anticipation.

I miss you very much.

Love Isabella.

CARTE POSTALE

Ce côté est exclusivement réservé à l'adresse

PAR AVION

Matthew Sedon
77 Sharea @___
Alexandria
Egypt

DES DÉPARTEMENTS D'OUTRE-MER
1946 CRÉATION
RÉPUBLIQUE FRANÇAISE

PARIS 26

Isabella

I can't begin to say how much more
alive I am on days when I receive a
card or a letter from you.

      Don't fret about the coming
year. You know the intensity of your
commitment—and so do your professors.
Who else in your class is already
halfway through their thesis?

      The masks were a disappointment.
They were early Nubian, but the
hieroglyphs on the concave had been
cut at a later date. The trip wasn't
wasted though—I made a few good
contacts.

      Flying back over Sudan I began
considering storming the cockpit and
demanding that the pilot take me to
Paris to see you. However I thought
better of it—I presume even the French
take a dim view of love-starved
hijackers.

Loads of love *Matthew*

ISABELLA de REIMS
343 RUE MASPERO
PARIS 75006
FRANCE

Matthew — Forgive my enigmatic introduction.
It's an old habit. Please allow me to begin afresh,
with a short summary of our first encounter.
 Late one night, my mother (who was midwife to
the Sicmon Islands) was called upon to preside over a birth,
and as neither assistant was to be found, I was enlisted as
temporary nurse. The baby, who made a fine
screaming and kicking entry into the world,
was you. In fact, my previous postcard shows
the young Master Sedon taking his first bath,
at the tender age of six days.
You've grown well Matty.
Now that we've been reintroduced, I was
wondering if I might prevail upon our old
aquaintanceship and ask you to pick up a
small package for us?
Many thanks
Sabine

Matthew Sedon
77 Sharea Otta
Alexandria
Egypt

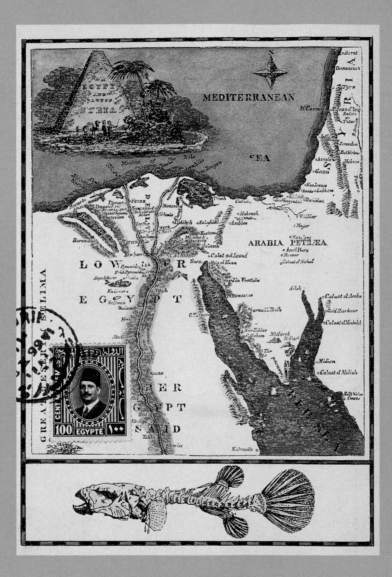

Sabine

Stone the crows, is that really what
I looked like? My parents didn't
leave behind any pictures of my early
childhood. It's quite eerie seeing
myself in such embryonic form. Thank
you for that unexpected gift—I'm in
your debt.

     Yes, I'd be more than happy to
pick up your package, presuming of
course that you can assure me I won't
be embarking on any illicit careers
like gunrunning or drug trafficking.

     Where will I find this parcel?
Somewhere in Alexandria, I hope.
Yours
     Matthew

SABINE STRoHE/

39 LA PAZ PL.

SAN RoSA

PAoLo

9T6

30522

Isabella
I have to confess that I'm slightly
distracted by another woman. A stranger who's
~~is~~ written to inform me that she was present
during my birth. I'm looking at one of her
postcards right now. Supposedly it shows me
as a baby. I've zero proof, but a voice in
my head keeps whispering that it is me.
Staring at myself as a newborn gives me an
odd sense of belonging, as if it confirmed
my existence—does that make any sense?

Anyway, this person, whose name is
Sabine Strohem, asked me to collect a
mysterious bunch of papers that I'm then
meant to read. I've no idea what they
contain, but I guess it can't do any harm.

I miss you. I love your eyes, and
your ever so slightly pointy ears. I miss
everything about you. I even miss your cat
making those funny noises under the bed.
Very yours   Matt

No 26   TYPES d'ÉGYPTIENNES,

ISABELLA de REIMS
343 RUE MASPERo
PARIS 75006
FRANCE

EGYPT
AIR MAIL
75 P. THOTMES III

My dear Matt

In the month since you were here this little
studio has become hugely empty.

Send me a copy of the baby picture, please.
I'm so curious to know what you looked
like when you were little. And yes, I
think I understand your fledgling
feelings of belonging.

I don't want to concern you but I've
been having more of those waking-
dreams and if anything they're
getting stronger. As I was reading
your card telling me about this

Sabine person, I saw her parcel full
of creatures, all scratching and
wriggling, trying desperately
to escape.

Attempting to keep up a long-distance
relationship is difficult enough, but
are you sure you want one with a woman
who is half-crazy? xx
                        Isabella

These ears are not pointy!

Matthew Solon
77 Florea Ola
Alexandria
Egypt

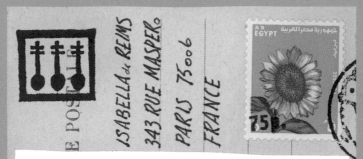

ISABELLA de REIMS
343 RUE MASPERO
PARIS 75006
FRANCE

Isabella
Of course I still want a relationship with
you—crazy or otherwise!

    I realize your visions must be
unsettling, but don't underestimate them,
the last one was right in a sense—the
parcel did contain something unusual.
Inside was a wooden box housing 65 cards
and letters, the massed correspondence
between Sabine and a man called Griffin
Moss. It's odd stuff. I'm trying to decide
if I've encountered an elaborate fiction,
or a series of events that, if true, cast
doubt over any concept of reality I've
ever held.

    The things that supposedly happened
between these two seem so unworldly. I
simply don't know what to make of it — in
a way, the whole correspondence, animal
images and all, looks as if they were
plucked from your dreams. I wish you could
see what I'm talking about.

    What I can't work out is, why the
hell does Sabine want *me*, of all people,
to read her mail?
Love you
               Matthew

THE PYRAMIDS AT GHIZEH

Sabine

I read the correspondence in the package. It's a strange story, and very convincing. For a while I almost believed it was for real. The plot had me hanging in the balance all the way. Though I must admit the last card left me confused—what's supposed to have happened in the end, do the characters ever meet? Or did their nemesis Frolatti find a way to shatter their tryst?

I hope you don't mind me asking questions about your story. Did you write it on your own? And did you invent Griffin, or is he in some part real? Why did you pick me to read your story? I'm a bone digger, not a literary critic.

Yours, in growing curiosity

Matthew

Where's Paolo? I've searched and it doesn't seem to exist.

SABINE STRoHEM
39 LA PAZ PL.
SAN RoSA
PAoLo 9T6

. . . than us. Indeed, in the early
. . . relationship Griffin believed he'd invented
me. He couldn't come to terms with my appearance at a
juncture when he badly needed a soulmate. He mistrusted
his own capacity to find what he was looking for. When I
entered his life he feared I was a black muse conjured from
his isolation. Only later, when he began to learn that the
inner-life manifests itself externally, did he understand
the fullness of who I was.
When he and I passed beyond the Pharos Arch in
Alexandria, we became as one. Yet we cannot return
through that golden mean without laying ourselves
open to Victor Frolatti and his kin. Many have suffered at
his hands but Frolatti's malevolence will never be assuaged.
Having failed to destroy Griffin and I, he and his Dark
Angels will undoubtedly wish to eradicate any further
opposition. We are forced to meet . . .

Carte postale Universelle.

Sabine

No, I do not understand. The mind (my mind) does not
accept such things easily. You tell me your
narrative is true, and maybe I believe you. I have
been steeped in Egyptology for most of my life. The
underworld is familiar territory to me, so I'm more
prepared to accept the unlikely than most people.

     But these proclamations of yours are
outlandish, and you can hardly blame my skepticism.
You are speaking as if you were recruiting me to
fight some universal force of evil straight from a
gothic novel. Are you really saying you believe that
there are such things as dark angels, or are you
just adding color to this tale of yours?

     I should make it clear that I have no
intention of being drawn into your intrigue.

Matthew

A place either exists or it doesn't. Where are you?

EGYPT
POST

75

Matthew

A universal force of evil?
If only it were that simple.
The balance of existence is more
delicate. An action to the left requires
a compensatory movement to the right
—the sun spins from the moon, the
King leans to the Queen. We each act
as an equilibrium.
Frolatti and his like are isolationists.
For them the rule of disinformation is
fundamental, but the gryphon keeps
moving and the tiny half-creatures
scuttle from side to side, trying not to
spill over the edges of the circle.
Insight, as always, is the key.
Don't worry about maps.
Your cards will find me.

Sabine

Matthew Sedon
77 Sharea Otta
Alexandria
Egypt

AIR M

A 3005452
40 ПАР
ПОЧТУ
40 ПАР

PER VIA AEREA
Mod. 24-R b

Isabella
Can't believe the things this Sabine woman has been
telling me. I'm way out of my depth and I won't
even begin to try and explain. I'm sending you
copies of all the cards and letters by secured
courier, and I'd really like to hear whether you
think I should be taking this seriously.

       Lately I've been getting a bit frustrated
because I can't contact you more easily. I know we
agreed that it would be more romantic to correspond
with postcards, and I know your laptop is on its
last legs, but I still wish you had e-mail. Are you
sure you won't consider letting me buy you a new
computer for your birthday? OK, OK, just thought
I'd give it a try—I don't want to infringe on your
independence.
Love
      Matthew

FOUND THIS OLD
GRYPHON CARD
IN THE MARKET.
ODD COINCIDENCE!

ISABELLA de REIMS
343 RUE MASPERo
PARIS 75oo6
FRANCE

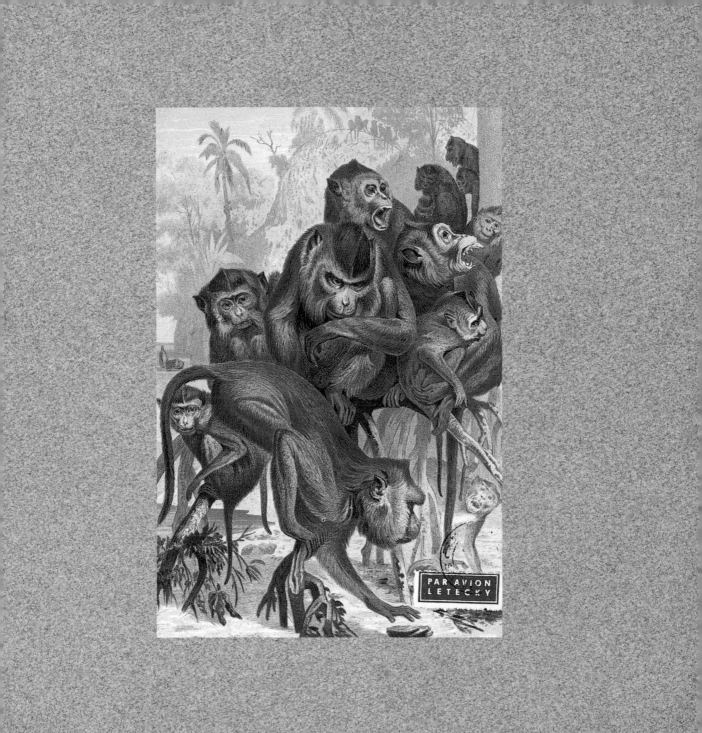

PAR AVION
LETECKY

Matthew — The courier arrived this morning and I've spent most of the day studying the 65 cards and letters along with copies of Sabine's messages to you. Should you take it seriously? Without question. I don't believe this is an elaborate trick, or the ravings of a lunatic. There's too much detail and anyway you are right: it echoes so many of the images from my waking dreams. I can even detect connections between the mythological animalization in their paintings, and

A. Bourdier — Versailles

my thesis on archaic zoology. These people see what I see and I want their help to understand what's happening to me.

And another thing — have you noticed the similarities between the two of them and us?

All my love
Isabella

Correspondance

BY AIR MAIL

CARTE POSTALE

Adresse

3,40 LA POSTE
RÉPUBLIQUE FRANÇAISE

Matthew Jadou
Flavel @ All
Alexandria
Egypt

Ms. de Reims, 343, rue Maspero, Paris 75006, France

Isabella

By now Matthew will have sent on the
various epistles that passed between
Sabine and myself. Hence you will
know a good deal about me. In turn,
I should tell you that we know much
about you, and I hope that our awareness
of your shadow-sight will not be of
alarm. You've carried this burdensome
gift for many years and I regret that we
are offering support so late in the day.
If you feel able to relate your most
recent dream to us, we would be happy
to help you put it into the larger context.
As for the other matter
that preoccupies you —
the barriers hindering
your yearnings for
Matthew are already
beginning to fall.
Yours
Griffin S Moss

I hope the cat is being well behaved.

1. *Apoderus longicollis.*
     gemmatus.
     ruticollis.

4. *Rhynchites Populi.*
5.   *pubescens.*
6.   *Collaris.*

Lizars sc.

Siberia.

Carolina.

England.

France.

Matt — No more than an hour after I posted my last missive to you, I received a card from Griffin Floss.

Apart from you, I've shared the secret of my day dreams with no one, yet he asks me about my "shadow-sight." Isn't that extraordinary?

Matty, will you write me a proper letter soon? These old cards we send one another are fine, but I need to know more about what's happening inside of you. I guess that reading letters has highlighted the way you and I glide over feelings. I haven't said anything before because I didn't want to frighten you away. Now I'm wondering if one or both of us are simply scared of any real intimacy.

XX Isabella

Matthew Sedom
33 Sharia Ahe
Alexandria
Egypt

Ce côté est exclusivement réservé à l'adresse.

CARTE POSTALE

AVION

RÉPUBLIQUE FRANÇAISE
EUROPA 3,00
FERRALI LE CHAT
LA POSTE 1997

Mr. Moss

I trust you, but I'm not sure why. Two mornings ago I witnessed the following:

A bird drops like a stone from the sun, past a silvery fogged-in moon, beyond pyramids of blazing scrolls, plunging downward into the desert. It pierces the sand's skin. Still diving, tunneling vertically, it burrows towards a great slumbering lion. The cat twists in his sleep, rubbing his nose with the back of his paw, unaware of the bird's approach. The earth holds her breath. It has turned cold and I hear grass rustling in the night wind. That is all.

In your correspondence with Sabine I see the same creatures that inhabit my visions. If you understand their significance, please tell me. What am I meant to do with these glimpses into another world?

Yours Isabella

Griffin Moss
39 La Paz pl.
San Rosa
Paolo

REPUBLIQUE FRANÇAISE 3.70

L'Égypte

POSTES ÉGYPTIENNES
ALEXANDRIE

POSTE LOCALE
Service Mixte
Taxe Ext.
Taxe Int.
TOTAL.

ISABELLA DE REIMS
343, RUE MASPERO
75006 PARIS
FRANCE

EGYPT
1998
AIR MAIL
RAMESSES III
75 P. POST DAY

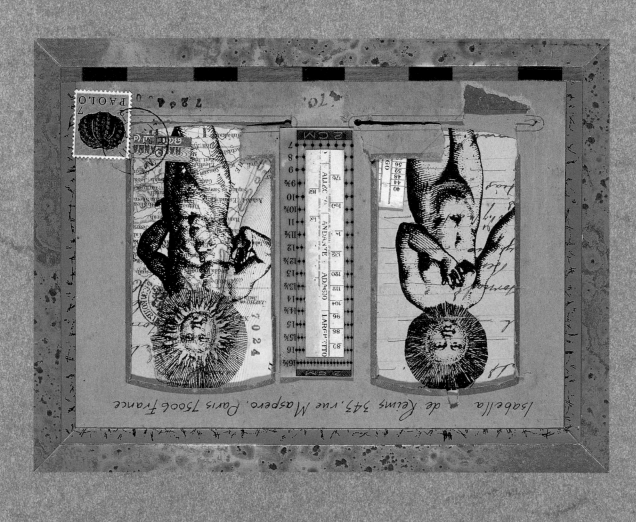

Matthew

Griffin sent me a letter in which he speaks of the alchemical teachings of Hermes Trismegistus. Also I noticed that Sabine invoked Mercury at the end of her letter to you.

You're the expert my dear. What do you know about Thoth, the Egyptian's version of Mercury? I've read that he was depicted as a baboon and an Ibis, but I haven't figured out if he's a friendly or hostile deity.

Matt, there's a rightness in all of this that I cannot describe. I keep thinking of a word from New Guinea — mokita. It means, "A truth everybody knows but knobody speaks". I think we are being asked to name a mokita.

It is dawning upon me, that our love has barely begun

and I am in awe. Your Isabella

Matthew Sexton
77 Sharea Orta
Alexandria
Egypt

Isabella
You offer so much of yourself. I wallow
in your words.

However things are not right here.
Someone broke into my apartment last
night. Nothing was taken but my papers
were left in disarray, and a couple of
them had strange scorch marks on their
edges. Security asked if I wanted the
gendarmes called in. I said, no. I didn't
want to get caught up in red tape. It was
almost certainly just a petty thief, and
yet I have this lingering sensation that
Sabine's world is closing around us.

I know that you want them to help
you interpret your visions, but I need to
tell Sabine that I'm not about to perform
whatever metaphysical balancing act they
have in mind for me.

To be honest, I don't trust any of
this, and I'm scared someone means us
real harm.

All my love, and much more. *Matt*

CARD

VIA AIR MAIL

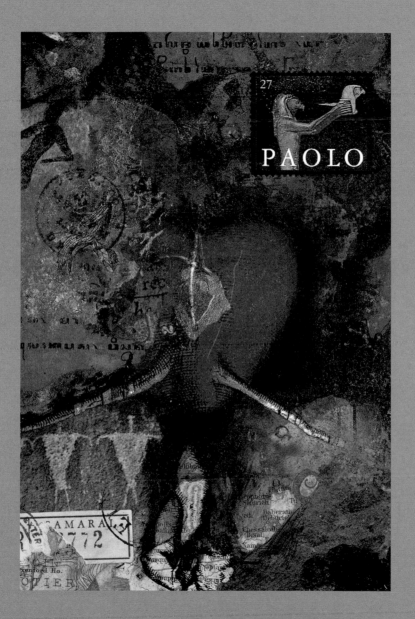

Matthew

I'm truly sorry, but you can't back out. You do not grasp the situation. I am not your mother— but we have been tied together from the moment of your birth and my spirit resides within you.

I understand all of this must be frightening and you want to pull away, protect yourself and Isabella, but that is not possible. Matthew, you already are me.

Matthew Sedon
77 Sharea Otto
Alexandria
Egypt

Sabine

Par Avion